Panda Big and Panda Small

Jane Cabrera

Panda Big and
Panda Small
do not like the
same things at all.

Panda Big likes to be **asleep** at the beginning of the day.

Panda Small is wide **awake** and wants to go and play!

Panda Big
likes to sit and
think at the
bottom
of these trees.

Panda
Small
is at the
top,
peeping
through
the leaves.

Panda Big likes to have her eyes **open** to watch the insects fly.

Panda
Small
has hers
shut
tight
when
bugs
come
dropping
by!

Panda Big
likes to eat
in front of
the bamboo.

Panda Small is there **behind,** playing peekaboo.

Panda Big likes to be **still** when lying on the ground.

"tickle tickle"

Panda Small just can't help **moving** noisily around.

Panda Big
likes to swing slowly
on the rope that's **long**.

Panda Small is on the **shorter rope.**
I hope she's hanging on!

Panda Big likes to stay **out** of the water, standing in the sun.

Panda Small has fallen **in** and thinks it's lots of fun.

But when **Panda Big** and **Panda Small** are **near** and

far

it makes them rather sad.
And then they know there's just one
thing that makes them **both** feel glad . . .

Being together.